Bella the Blueberry Fairy

Faye the Forest Fairy

Evie the Strawberry Fairy

Brightwing Butterfly

Sophie, Queen of the Fairies

The illustrations in this book are hand-drawn using pencils, watercolour paint, pastels and gouache.

Translated by Polly Lawson. First published in German as *Erdbeerinchen Erdbeerfee. Erdbeerzauber im Feenland*
by Arena Verlag GmbH 2014. First published in English by Floris Books in 2019
Story and illustrations © 2014 Stefanie Dahle. English version © 2019 Floris Books
All rights reserved. No part of this publication may be reproduced without
the prior permission of Floris Books, Edinburgh www.florisbooks.co.uk
British Library CIP data available ISBN 978-178250-594-5
Printed in China through Asia Pacific Offset Ltd

Evie the Strawberry Fairy

Evie and the Strawberry Balloon Ride

Stefanie Dahle

Floris
Books

"Look!" called Evie the Strawberry Fairy, "Faye the Forest Fairy is holding a strawberry fair. There's even a competition!"

"Ooh!" Brightwing Butterfly fluttered with excitement. "You're a strawberry expert, Evie. Maybe you'll win!"

Evie had a busy few days rushing about her teapot house:
up and down the ladder, and to and fro in the kitchen.
It made Brightwing Butterfly dizzy.

On the morning of the fair, Brightwing asked Evie what she
was entering for the competition.

"I'm baking my scrumptious strawberry cake!" she said.

"Hmm," said Brightwing. "Is a cake special enough to win?"

Evie's eyes twinkled. "I've also got a big surprise!"

Just then there was a knock on the door. It was Sophie, Queen of the Fairies.

"Hello, Evie," said Sophie. "I've told my little cousin Bella that you're lots of fun. Can she play with you today?"

Evie smiled. "Bella, we're going to the strawberry fair. Would you like to come?"

"Yes, please!" Bella cried.

Evie scampered up the ladder to the lid
of her teapot house. Bella and Brightwing
followed, and couldn't believe their eyes!

"Evie, it's wonderful!" gasped Brightwing.

"This is my surprise entry for the fair,"
said Evie. "A strawberry hot-air balloon!"

"How did you make it?" asked Bella,
gazing up in wonder.

"I've been working hard since we saw
that poster! I stitched together fabric from my
old strawberry tent and tied it to a big, old
laundry basket," Evie explained. "Now,
let's go on a strawberry balloon ride!"

They floated along happily until Brightwing Butterfly suddenly shouted, "Watch out for that tree!"

Oh, squashed-up strawberries! It was too late! The balloon snagged on a branch and stuck fast. Evie and Bella tumbled out of the basket into a robin's nest.

"I'm glad you dropped in," said the surprised robin. "I've been sitting alone resting, tired from lining my nest with grass."

"We'll help!" said Evie. She and Bella climbed down and gathered big handfuls of straw.

"Oh, thank you!" twittered the robin. "But how will you get to the strawberry fair? I could fly you to the river."

"Yes, please!" said Evie. "I wish we still had the balloon, but let's go and enter the cake."

At the riverside, they said goodbye and thank you to the robin.
"Are you going to the strawberry fair?" asked a small
squeaky voice. "Step on board my wonderful boat!"
"Who said that?" asked Brightwing, looking around.

Then they saw a teeny-tiny pixie.

"Oh, I'm so small no one notices me!" sighed the pixie.
"If only I stood out a bit more..."

"I'll help!" exclaimed Evie. She touched her magic wand to
the pixie's hat, and it turned scarlet as a strawberry! He was delighted.

The pixie took them over the river to the meadow, where they said goodbye and thank you.

"Thief! Thief!" cried a deep voice. It was an old hare.

"What's happened?" asked Evie. "You look hopping mad!"

"A naughty mouse stole my lunch!" the hare sighed. "Oh, I'm so hungry."

"We'll help!" said Evie. She took the strawberry cake out of her bag, Bella handed it to the grateful hare, and they said goodbye.

They hurried on, but suddenly Evie stopped.
    "Now I don't have my cake, or my hot-air balloon.
I have nothing to enter into the competition!"
She frowned and sat down heavily.

"It's a shame, Evie," said Brightwing.
"But the fair will be fun anyway."
"Please let's go, please!" said Bella.
"Oh, alright," agreed Evie reluctantly.

As they arrived at the strawberry fair everyone was chattering with excitement. Faye the Forest Fairy glimmered under the lanterns in her green dress.

"Welcome everyone!" she called. "Evie, you're just in time. Quick, take a number!"

"I'm sorry, I don't have anything—" Evie tried to explain.

But Faye kept talking. "Thank you all for coming. Let's start the competition!"

First was a small, furry troll with a strawberry pudding placed on a spinning top. The pudding whirled so fast that everyone was splattered with strawberry sauce!

"Er, very... unusual!" called Faye politely. "Who's next?"

Three bumblebees dressed as strawberries performed a beautiful dance. There was a snail disguised as a strawberry, a fairy with a strawberry cart, and an elf who hopped around on a big strawberry-shaped bouncy ball.

"He's so funny!" Bella giggled.

But Evie just sighed.

Then Faye turned to her. "You're next, are you ready?"

The strawberry fairy's eyes filled with tears. "I'm sorry, I can't enter. My hot-air balloon got stuck and I gave my cake to a hungry hare."

"And that was very kind of you," called a deep voice. "It was delicious!"

Everybody whirled around in surprise.

It was the hare, the robin and the pixie – and they had
brought Evie's strawberry hot-air balloon with them!
"We rescued your balloon to say thank you for helping us,"
said the hare.

Everyone cooed with wonder.

"Evie, your balloon is beautiful!" cried Faye. "And you have been kind and generous too. You deserve first prize!"

Evie was thrilled! She climbed on top of the tree-trunk podium and Faye placed a gold medal around her neck.

The dancing bees won second place, and the bouncing elf came third.

Once it was all over, Evie, Bella and Brightwing Butterfly climbed into the balloon's basket and floated across the sky, back to Evie's teapot house.

Evie's little insect friends welcomed her.
"It's so lovely to be home!" Evie smiled.
"The fair was lovely, but now I just want to take
care of my strawberry plants."
"Did you enjoy yourself, Bella?" asked Brightwing.

"It was the best fun ever!" cried Bella. "Especially when Evie got splattered with pudding sauce," she added cheekily.

"Mmm, pudding. Who's hungry?" asked Evie.

"Me! Me!" cried Bella.

They finished their day with a happy sticky supper, helping themselves to toast and Evie's home-made strawberry jam.